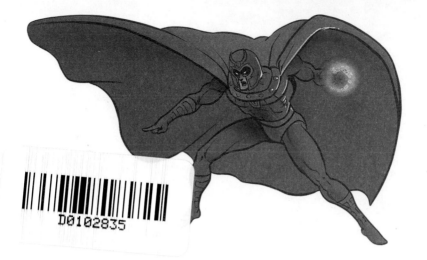

A NOTE TO PARENTS

When your children are ready to "step into reading," giving them the right books—and lots of them—is as crucial as giving them the right food to eat. **Step into Reading Books** present exciting stories and information reinforced with lively, colorful illustrations that make learning to read fun, satisfying, and worthwhile. They are priced so that acquiring an entire library of them is affordable. And they are beginning readers with an important difference—they're written on four levels.

Step 1 Books, with their very large type and extremely simple vocabulary, have been created for the very youngest readers. **Step 2 Books** are both longer and slightly more difficult. **Step 3 Books,** written to mid-second-grade reading levels, are for the child who has acquired even greater reading skills. **Step 4 Books** offer exciting nonfiction for the increasingly proficient reader.

Children develop at different ages. **Step into Reading Books,** with their four levels of reading, are designed to help children become good—and interested—readers *faster*. The grade levels assigned to the four steps—preschool through grade 1 for Step 1, grades 1 through 3 for Step 2, grades 2 and 3 for Step 3, and grades 2 through 4 for Step 4—are intended only as guides. Some children move through all four steps very rapidly; others climb the steps over a period of several years. These books will help your child "step into reading" in style!

Library of Congress Cataloging-in-Publication Data:
Enter Magneto / based on teleplays by Mark Edward Edens ; adapted by Eric Weiner ; illustrated by
Aristides Ruiz and Dana and Del Thompson. p. cm. — (Step into reading. A Step 3 book) At head
of title: X-Men. SUMMARY: Professor Xavier and his mutant X-Men battle the evil Magneto at a missile
base and at a chemical plant.
ISBN: 0-679-86043-6 (trade pbk.) — ISBN 0-679-96043-0 (lib. bdg.)
[1. Heroes—Fiction. 2. Science fiction.] I. Edens, Mark Edward. II. Ruiz, Aristides, ill. III.
Thompson, Dana, ill. IV. Thompson, Del, ill. V. Title. VI. Series: Step into reading. Step 3 book.
PZ7. W43636En 1994 [Fic]—dc20 93-41027

Manufactured in the United States of America 10 9 8 7 6 5 4 3 2 1
STEP INTO READING is a trademark of Random House, Inc.

Step into Reading™

X-MEN®

Enter Magneto

based on teleplays by Mark Edward Edens
adapted by Eric Weiner
cover illustration by Dana and Del Thompson
illustrated by Aristides Ruiz

A Step 3 Book

Random House 🏠 New York

1
The Missile Crisis

At the X-Men's secret hideout, two mutants were fighting.

Cyclops shot an energy beam at Wolverine. Wolverine ducked.

Then Wolverine charged Cyclops. Cyclops fell. Wolverine jumped on top of him.

Wolverine growled. Then he raised his three sharp claws high.

Wolverine and Cyclops heard someone
clapping. They stopped fighting at once.

Professor Xavier came toward them.
"Good work, Wolverine," he said.

"You're lucky, Cyclops," Wolverine
said. "I almost forgot this was a practice
fight."

Wolverine helped Cyclops up. They were part of a team now. They were X-Men.

Professor X was the leader of the X-Men. He had started Xavier's School for Gifted Youngsters to help mutants learn how to control their powers.

Professor X hoped that his students would use their powers for the benefit of humankind.

They were about to get their chance.

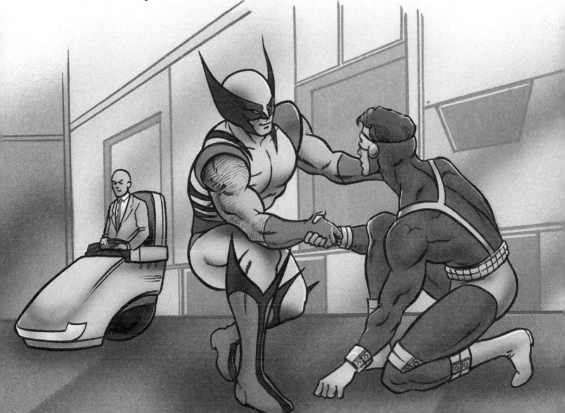

"WARNING! WARNING!" boomed the computer's voice. "A NUCLEAR MISSILE BASE IS UNDER ATTACK!"

Professor X was calm.

"Gentlemen," he said, "practice is over.
Now it is time for a *real* test of your
powers!"

Meanwhile, at the missile base, a battle was raging.

Hundreds of soldiers were shooting their laser guns. Twenty tanks were firing their cannons.

They were all firing at one evil mutant. His name was Magneto.

The blasts didn't bother Magneto at all. He just laughed.

"You think you can stop *me?*" he roared. "No one can stop Magneto!"

Magneto used his magnetic power to pull all the bolts out of the tanks. The tanks fell to pieces.

The same magnetic power pulled all the guns out of the soldiers' hands.

The guns came together in a giant SMASH!

The soldiers ran for their lives.

Magneto headed for the missile control tower.

WHOOSH!

Something flew over Magneto's head.

It was the X-Men's speedy jet, the Blackbird!

The Blackbird landed in a cloud of dust. The hatch opened.

Cyclops, Wolverine, and Storm jumped out.

"Well, if it isn't Professor Xavier's students," said Magneto. "I've been watching you. Trying to help the humans, eh? Fools! Don't you know that humans will always hate us mutants? And why? Just because we're different!"

Magneto started toward the missile control tower again.

Cyclops blocked his way.

"What are you going to do?" Cyclops asked.

"Get rid of all the humans," Magneto said. "Then I will rule the world. And it will be safe for mutants."

Storm raised her arms. Lightning bolts flew in all directions. Thunder boomed.

"The X-Men will not let that happen!" she said.

Magneto said nothing. But he closed his outstretched hand.

Storm, Wolverine, and Cyclops were trapped in a magnetic bubble.

Magneto used his power to lift the X-Men high into the air. Then he smashed them into the ground.

Cyclops was the first to recover.

"Wolverine! Storm!" he called out. "Are you all right?"

"Like new," growled Wolverine.

"Nothing is broken," said Storm.

Just then they heard a grinding noise. The missile silos were opening.

"The missiles!" Storm cried.

Cyclops blasted a hole through the wall of the missile control building.

"This way!" he shouted.

Storm, Cyclops, and Wolverine went into the missile control room.

The room was filled with computers. But there were no people.

"TEN...NINE..." said a computer.

"The missiles are set to fire in ten seconds!" Cyclops said.

"EIGHT...SEVEN..." said the computer.

"Each missile could blow up a city," said Storm.

"SIX..." said the computer.

SNIKT! Wolverine's claws sprang out.

"FIVE...FOUR..." said the computer.

He sliced the computers to ribbons.

But the computer voice kept counting down. "THREE...TWO...ONE!"

"No!" shouted Cyclops.

"IGNITION," called the computer.

There was a loud rumble. The rumble became a roar. And three nuclear missiles flew into the sky.

"I know what I must do," said Storm. She flew after the missiles. She flew faster and faster.

"She's going to blow up those missiles before they land!" said Wolverine.

"Yes," said Cyclops. "But she could be killed at the same time."

Back at the mansion, Professor X used his telepathic powers to speak to Storm. "There is another way to stop the missiles," he told her.

Storm listened to the Professor's voice in her mind. She knew what to do.

She raised her arms. A whirlwind began to blow. The strong wind blew the missiles into the sea.

2
Who Is Magneto?

Cyclops, Storm, and Wolverine returned to the mansion. Professor X told the X-Men about Magneto.

"I have fought Magneto before," the Professor said with a sigh. "But many years ago, he was a good friend. We worked together in a hospital during the war. No one knew we were mutants. We both used our powers secretly to save as many lives as we could."

"Then Magneto's family was killed in the war. Magneto became angry and blamed all humans.

"I tried to talk to him then. I wanted him to help me teach humans to live in peace with mutants.

"I will never forget his words: 'Humans can't even live in peace with each other.'"

Professor X looked sad.

"Magneto will strike again soon," he said. "But where?"

3
X-Men to the Rescue

The next morning, a guard at the
Krone chemical factory was watching TV.
"Yesterday, a group of mutants
attacked a nuclear missile base," said the

TV news announcer. "As you can see, the base was destroyed. But the mutants failed to set off any missiles."

"Those evil mutants," the guard said. "Good thing they never come near this place."

Just then, all the screws came flying
out of his TV set.

The guard looked up.

It was Magneto.

The guard screamed.

Magneto marched on through the chemical plant. He used his magnetic power to break pipes everywhere.

Dangerous chemicals poured out of the broken pipes. Guards and factory workers ran for their lives.

Suddenly four figures came toward Magneto. They were Cyclops, Storm, Wolverine, and Rogue.

"Again, only the children!" said Magneto. "When will Xavier show his face?"

"Sorry to disappoint you, Magneto," Cyclops said. "You'll have to make do with *us!*"

Cyclops blasted Magneto with an energy beam.

But Magneto hid himself in a magnetic bubble. Cyclops's beam bounced right off.

Then Storm raised her arms. Lightning bolts flew out.

The lightning hit Magneto in the chest. But Magneto just laughed.

"You forget, Storm. Electricity is *good* for magnets."

"Maybe we can steal some of this old boy's thunder," Rogue said to Wolverine.

Together, Rogue and Wolverine raced toward Magneto.

But Magneto caught them both in a magnetic net. He threw them hard against the wall.

The wall cracked. Chunks of plaster rained down on Cyclops, Storm, Wolverine, and Rogue.

"You have wasted enough of my time," said Magneto. "If the Professor is too afraid to face me, you must pay the price."

Using his magnetic power, he raised a huge vat of acid over the fallen X-Men.

"Stop," said a voice.

Magneto turned.

It was Professor X.

"It's me you want," the Professor said. "Let them go."

Magneto smiled. "Charles," he said, "it's been so long."

"You must end this madness,

Magneto," said the Professor. "You are
hurting innocent people."

"No humans are innocent," Magneto
said. "I'll give you one last chance. Join me
in my fight."

"Never," said Professor X.

"Then you will be the first to go," said
Magneto.

Magneto threw the vat of acid at Professor X. But the Professor quickly moved out of the way.

Then Magneto used his magnetic power to turn over the Professor's hoverchair. It was made of metal!

The Professor fell to the ground.

Professor X had lost the use of his legs the last time he fought Magneto. Now he couldn't stand. He dragged himself across the floor with his arms.

"Farewell, Charles," Magneto said. He raised his hand to blast the Professor. "I'm sorry to see you go. You were the best of us."

Professor X used all his telepathic power to enter Magneto's mind.

He forced Magneto to remember the war.

Magneto saw bombs falling. He saw his loved ones dying.

"No! No!" he shouted, unable to bear the memories any longer. He had to escape them.

He blasted a hole in the factory wall
and flew away.

4
Magneto's Challenge

That night, Storm found the Professor in the War Room of the mansion. He looked very sad.

"The last time I faced Magneto," he said, "I had a chance to finish him off. But I didn't. I couldn't. And now he's back. And stronger than ever."

"He may be strong," said Storm, "but you are stronger."

"This time I tricked him," said Professor X. "But I fear for the future."

Magneto looked out to sea.
His cape flew out behind him.
Moonlight shone off his helmet.
"We will meet again, Xavier," he said.
"And next time…"